Impossible Pets

story by

Richard Morecroft

and

Alison Mackay

pictures by

Wayne Harris

ABC
Books

To Margaret Wild and David Francis,
thanks for your enthusiasm — R.M. & A.M.

To Pete and Moshi and Babs — W.H.

  The ABC 'Wave' device and the 'ABC For Kids' device are
trademarks of the Australia Broadcasting Corporation and are
used under licence by HarperCollins*Publishers* Australia.

First published in 1999 by ABC Books for the
AUSTRALIAN BROADCASTING CORPORATION.
Reprinted by HarperCollins*Publishers* Australia Pty Limited
ABN 36 009 913 517
www.harpercollins.com.au

HarperCollins*Publishers*
25 Ryde Road, Pymble, Sydney, NSW 2073, Australia
31 View Road, Glenfield, Auckland 0627, New Zealand
A 53, Sector 57, Noida, UP, India
77–85 Fulham Palace Road, London W6 8JB, United Kingdom
2 Bloor Street East, 20th floor, Toronto, Ontario M4W 1A8, Canada
10 East 53rd Street, New York NY 10022, USA

National Library of Australia
Cataloguing-in-Publication entry
Morecroft, Richard.
Impossible pets.
ISBN 9780 7333 0704 3. (Hardback)
ISBN 9780 7333 0704 1. (Paperback)
I. Mackay, Alison. 1966—. II. Harris, Wayne.
III. Australian Broadcasting Corporation. IV Title.
A823.3

The illustrations were drawn with graphite pencil
and painted with watercolour.
Set in Jimbo and Sassoon Sans Slope
Designed and typeset by Monkeyfish
Colour separations by Leo Reprographics
Printed in China by Everbest Printing Co. Ltd.

6 5 4   10 11 12 13

Nerissa wanted
a pet — a pet of
her very own.
So one day she
brought home a
polar bear.

'How lovely!' said her parents.

'What soft, white fur,' said her mother.

'Note the huge paws designed for walking across snow and ice,' said her father.

'His name is Jeremy,' said Nerissa.

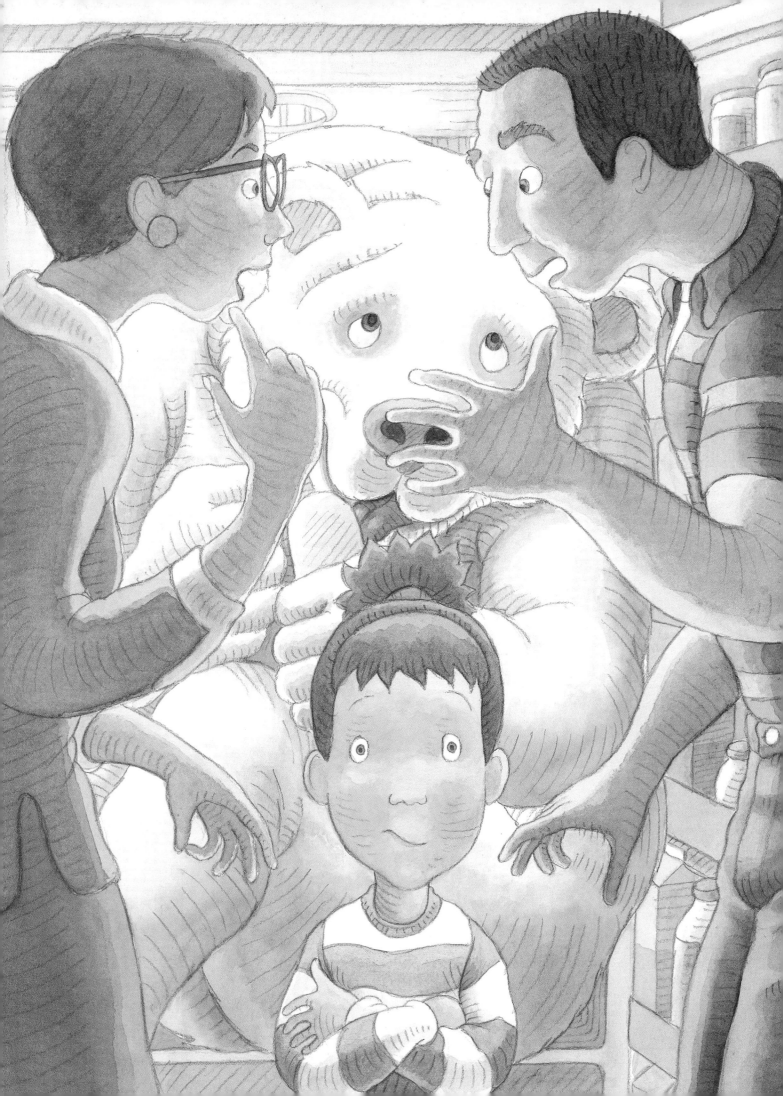

Unfortunately, as soon as the fridge door was open, Jeremy climbed inside.

'Don't worry,' said Nerissa's father. 'Everything is under control!'

But it wasn't. Nobody could use the fridge. The next day, the polar bear had to go.

Nerissa still wanted a pet. So she brought home an anaconda.

'How lovely!' said her parents.

'What beautifully patterned skin,' said her mother.

'Note how the eyes are set high on the head so the snake can hide under water while it watches for prey,' said her father.

'Her name is Margaret,' said Nerissa.

Unfortunately, there was a misunderstanding when her father went to have a bath.

'No problem,' he said. 'Everything is under control!'

But it wasn't. It took all six of the Santo brothers from next door to untangle him from Margaret.

The next day, the anaconda had to go.

Nerissa still wanted a pet. So she brought home a herd of wildebeest.

'How lovely!' said her parents.

'They can all play together,' said her mother.

'Are they gnu or second-hand?' asked her father. (He enjoyed a little joke.)

'This is Harrison,' said Nerissa, 'and Rosy and Sarah and Christopher and John and Julie ... ' Nerissa introduced all the wildebeest, which were happily eating the shrubs.

'They seem well under control,' said her father.

But they weren't, because the next day they decided to migrate south as they always did at that time of year. It caused rather a problem on the highway.

The wildebeest didn't have to go, but they'd gone anyway.

Still Nerissa didn't have a pet. So she brought home a vulture.

'How lovely!' said her parents.

'What glossy black feathers,' said her mother.

'Note the strong hooked beak for tearing meat,' said her father.

'His name is Mortimer,' said Nerissa.

Unfortunately, there was an argument at the dinner table over the roast leg of lamb.

'Never fear,' said her father. 'Everything is under control!'

But it wasn't. The vulture was perched on top of the television and so was the lamb roast.

'Oh well,' said Nerissa's father, 'perhaps Mortimer just wanted a TV dinner!'

The next day, the vulture had to go.

Nerissa wanted a pet more than ever. So she brought home a Komodo dragon.

'How lovely!' said her parents.

'What beautiful brown eyes,' said her mother.

'Note the ability to move surprisingly fast,' said her father, as the neighbour's poodle, Mitzi, barked at the Komodo dragon. Just once.

'Don't panic!' said Nerissa's father. 'Everything is under control!'

But it wasn't, and Mrs Garble,
the neighbour, was quite upset.
The Komodo dragon had to go.
Immediately.

'Her name was Charlotte,'
said Nerissa.

The next day, while Nerissa was playing in the garden,
a spaceship came down through the clouds.

It was driven by an alien called Zox. He wanted a pet — a pet of his very own — so he took Nerissa back to his planet.

'How lovely!' said Zox's parents.

'So nice and small,' said his mother.

'Note the ten fingers and only two eyes,' said his father.

'Her name is ZZgrrrK,' said Zox.

'No it's not!' shouted Nerissa.

'Don't be alarmed, everyone,' said Zox's father. 'Everything is under control!'

But it wasn't. Nerissa stuck out her tongue, pushed over a robot, and kicked Zox's father rather hard on one of his tentacles. So the next day, Nerissa had to go.

Zox delivered
Nerissa back to her
garden.

'How well you look!'
said her mother.

'Note the silent anti-
gravity drive on the alien
ship,' said her father.

'What's your friend's
name?' asked her mother.

'I call him Howard,' said
Nerissa.

As the spaceship disappeared
into the clouds, her father said,
'What a relief! Everything is
under control again.'

And it was.

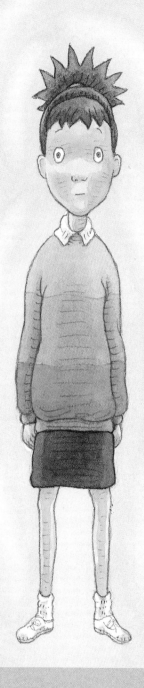

Nerissa still didn't have a pet
— but at least she wasn't one.